THIS WALKER BOOK BELONGS TO:

_____

_____

_____

_____

For David Davies

First published 1985 by Walker Books Ltd
87 Vauxhall Walk, London SE11 5HJ

This edition published 2005 for Index Books Ltd

2 4 6 8 10 9 7 5 3 1

© 1985 Shirley Hughes

The right of Shirley Hughes to be identified as author/illustrator of this work
has been asserted by her in accordance with the Copyright, Designs and Patents Act 1988

This book has been typeset in Vendome

Printed in China

British Library Cataloguing in Publication Data: a catalogue record for this book
is available from the British Library

ISBN 0-7445-6985-0

www.walkerbooks.co.uk

When We Went to the Park

Shirley Hughes

WALKER BOOKS
AND SUBSIDIARIES

LONDON · BOSTON · SYDNEY · AUCKLAND

When Grandpa and I
put on our coats

and went

to the park ...

We saw one black cat
sitting on a wall,

Two big girls
licking ice-creams,

Three ladies chatting

on a bench,

Four babies
in buggies,

Five children playing

in the sand-pit,

Six runners running,

Seven dogs chasing one another,

Eight boys
kicking a ball,

Nine ducks
swimming on the pond,

Ten birds swooping
in the sky,

and so many leaves that I
couldn't count them all.

On the way back we saw
the black cat again.

Then we went
home for tea.

WALKER BOOKS

The Nursery Collection

SHIRLEY HUGHES says that she found working on The Nursery Collection "very stimulating". They were her first books for very young children and she remarks that creating them was "concentrated and exhausting because it was like actually being with a very small child." The brother and sister featured in the books reappear in her book of seasonal verse *Out and About* and in a series of books about "doing words" – *Bouncing*, *Chatting*, *Giving* and *Hiding* – now collected in a single volume as *Let's Join In*.

Shirley Hughes has won numerous awards, including the Kate Greenaway Medal for *Dogger* and the Eleanor Farjeon Award for services to children's literature. In 1999 she was awarded the OBE. Among her many popular books are the *Alfie and Annie Rose*, *Lucy and Tom* and *Tales of Trotter Street* series.

Shirley and her husband, a retired architect, have lived in the same house in west London for more than forty years. They have three grown-up children and six grandchildren.

ISBN 0-7445-6983-4 (pb)   ISBN 0-7445-6986-9 (pb)   ISBN 0-7445-6984-2 (pb)   ISBN 0-7445-6981-8 (pb)   ISBN 0-7445-6985-0 (pb)   ISBN 0-7445-6982-6 (pb)